Ladybird  Readers

The Silver Ring

Series Editor: Sorrel Pitts
Story by Catherine Baker
Illustrated by Chris Jevons

Ladybird Readers Starter Level

Title		Phonics	Sight Words
1	Alphabet Book	A—Z	
2	Is it Nat?	s a t p i n	a is it
3	Nat Sits		an in sit
4	Top Dog and Pompom	m d g o c k	and can I into no
5	Top Dog is Sick		got not
6	The Fun Run	e u r h b f l	at get go has off the to up
7	Gus is Hot!		full his of on put
8	Jazz the Vet	j v w x y z qu	be but had he him she tell was
9	Vick the Vet		did well will
10	Dash and Thud	ch sh th ng	if ran then they with yes
11	Big Bad Bash		big long that this
12	The Big Fish	ai ee oa oo	her look see them
13	The Big Ship		let me my too
14	Martin and Lorna	ar or ur ow oi er	all are for
15	Farmer Carl		cut down good help now
16	The Big Dipper	igh ear air ure	as have like said some went you
17	The Silver Ring		come from so stop we what

First, go through the phonemes on page 4, and do the activity on page 5. Then, read the words in the first half of the book, focusing on pronunciation and blending.

The sight words are introduced in the second half of the book, first on their own and then in full sentences.

At the back of the book, there are activities and assessments practicing phonemes and sight words. These icons indicate the key skills required in each activity:

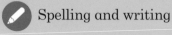 Spelling and writing   Speaking   Reading

Ladybird Readers

The Silver Ring

Look at the story

First, look at the words and pictures.
Use the words to practice phonics.

Phonics focus

igh   ear   air   ure

lights

night

beard

gears

near

chair

stairs

fair

secure

Aa Bb Cc Dd Ee Ff Gg Hh Ii Jj Kk Ll M

Activity

1 **Circle all the words with the sound *ear*.**

(near)

chair

fair

gears

beard

secure

night

beard

chair

stairs

secure

fair

near

night

beard

gears

Ladybird Readers

The Silver Ring

Read the story

Now, read the story in full sentences.
Practice using the sight words.

Sight words

come

from

so

stop

we

what

"Come and see the town from up high on the Silver Ring!" said a man with a beard.

All the pods have some chairs in them.

Mark, Dad, and Mitch go up the stairs and into a pod.

The man checks the door is secure, and off they go!

Up high, Mark sees the lights from the fair.

"Look, that is a church," said Dad.

"And I can see the park," said Mitch.

They are in a pod near the top. Bang!

The Silver Ring stops!

They wait and wait.

"We might be in this pod
all night," said Mitch.

"We might be in it for years and years!" said Mark.

The man with the beard
checks the gears. The gears
need oil.

So, he gets a can of oil.
The Silver Ring turns!

Down come Mark, Dad, and Mitch.

The man tugs the door. Mom cheers!

Activities

Write the words in the correct boxes

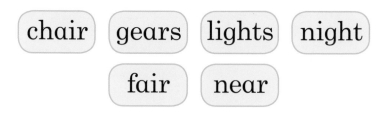

chair   gears   lights   night

fair   near

igh	ear	air
		chair

3 **Find the sight words.**

come   from   stop   so   what   we

c	o	m	e	s	w
t	f	a	l	t	h
e	r	r	h	o	a
s	o	u	g	p	t
k	m	w	e	j	r

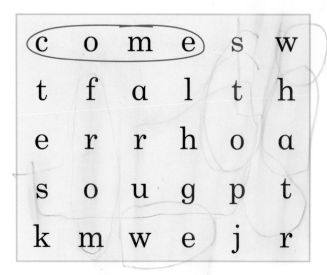

Assessment

4 **Look and read.**
Write the correct letters. 📖 ✏️

| igh | ear | air | ure | igh |

1 "We might be in this pod all n igh t."

2 The man checks the door is sec＿＿＿＿.

3 Mark sees the l＿＿＿ts from the fun fair.

4 Mark, Dad, and Mitch go up the st＿＿＿s.

5 The g＿＿＿s need oil.

5 Circle the correct sight words.

1  **"Come** / **"Some** and see the town."

2  **So,** / **Co,** he gets a can of oil.

3  **"Wat** / **"What** was that?"

4  The Silver Ring **stopps!** / **stops!**

5  **"We** / **"Wi** will get down in the end."

6  Mark sees the lights **frum** / **from** the fair.

Starter

Starter 1

Alphabet Book

978–0–241–39367–3

Starter 2

Is it Nat?

978–0–241–39368–0

Starter 3

Nat Sits

978–0–241–39369–7

Starter 4

Top Dog and Pompom

978–0–241–39370–3

Starter 5

Top Dog is Sick

978–0–241–39371–0

Starter 6

The Fun Run

978–0–241–39372–7

Starter 7

Gus is Hot!

978–0–241–39373–4

Starter 8

Jazz the Vet

978–0–241–39374–1

Starter 9

Vick the Vet

978–0–241–39375–8

Starter 10

Dash and Thud

978–0–241–39376–5

Starter 11

Big Bad Bash

978–0–241–39377–2

Starter 12

The Big Fish

978–0–241–39379–6

Starter 13

The Big Ship

978–0–241–39380–2

Starter 14

Martin and Lorna

978–0–241–39381–9

Starter 15

Farmer Carl

978–0–241–39382–6

Starter 16

The Big Dipper

978–0–241–39383–3

Starter 17

The Silver Ring

978–0–241–39384–0

LADYBIRD BOOKS

UK | USA | Canada | Ireland | Australia
India | New Zealand | South Africa

Ladybird Books is part of the Penguin Random House group of companies
whose addresses can be found at global.penguinrandomhouse.com.
www.penguin.co.uk   www.puffin.co.uk   www.ladybird.co.uk

**Penguin
Random House
UK**

First published 2017. This edition published 2019
001

Copyright © Ladybird Books Ltd, 2017

Printed in China

A CIP catalogue record for this book is available from the British Library

ISBN: 978-0-241-39384-0

All correspondence to:
Ladybird Books
Penguin Random House Children's
80 Strand, London WC2R 0RL